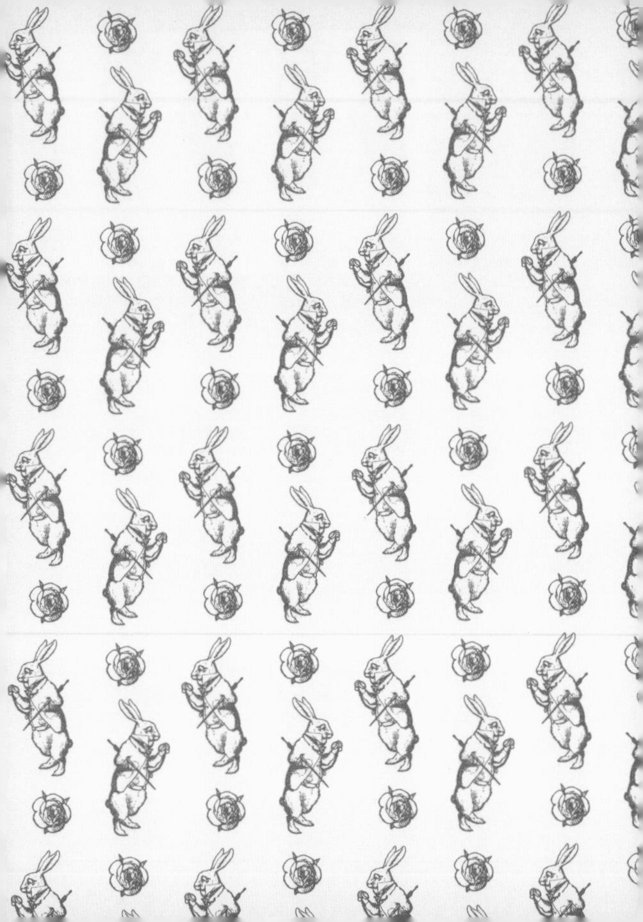

THE MACMILLAN ALICE

EVERLASTING DIARY

THE MACMILLAN

ALICE

EVERLASTING DIARY

With quotations from Lewis Carroll's
Alice's Adventures in Wonderland
And *Through the Looking-Glass*

Illustrations by Sir John Tenniel

Macmillan

Alice's Adventures in Wonderland and *Through the Looking-Glass and What Alice Found There*, written by Lewis Carroll with illustrations by Sir John Tenniel, were first published by Macmillan & Co. Ltd, 1865 and 1872

The Macmillan Alice Everlasting Diary first published 2015
by Macmillan Children's Books, an imprint of Pan Macmillan,
20 New Wharf Road, London N1 9RR
Associated companies throughout the world

www.panmacmillan.com

ISBN 978-1-50981-042-0

1 3 5 7 9 10 8 6 4 2

A CIP catalogue record for this book is available from the British Library

Printed in China

"I began dealing with your house with full confidence in it in every way – and that confidence is undiminished."

Lewis Carroll writes to Alexander Macmillan
in April, 1871

Introduction

A century and a half after its original publication, Lewis Carroll's Wonderland continues to fascinate us. Brave, curious and strong-minded Alice, the anxious White Rabbit, the unique Mad Hatter, are universally beloved. What is it about Alice and her friends that has kept them in our hearts and our thoughts for 150 years?

The quotations in this everlasting diary act as an introduction to the fanciful world and fantastic language of Carroll's books, and perhaps will lead you to discover the original stories for yourself.

You may decide to use this book as a birthday book, to record birthdays and anniversaries. Or perhaps you could follow Humpty Dumpty's advice, and use it to record un-birthdays . . .

Humpty Dumpty's Advice

From Chapter Six, *Through the Looking-Glass and What Alice Found There*

"They gave it to me," Humpty Dumpty continued thoughtfully... "they gave it me—for an un-birthday present."

"I beg your pardon?" Alice said with a puzzled air.

"I'm not offended," said Humpty Dumpty.

"I mean, what is an un-birthday present?"

"A present given when it isn't your birthday, of course."

Alice considered a little. "I like birthday presents best," she said at last.

"You don't know what you're talking about!" cried Humpty Dumpty. "How many days are there in a year?"

"Three hundred and sixty-five," said Alice.

"And how many birthdays have you?"

"One."

"And if you take one from three hundred and sixty-five, what remains?"

"Three hundred and sixty-four, of course."

Humpty Dumpty looked doubtful. "I'd rather see that done on paper," he said.

Alice couldn't help smiling as she took out her memorandum-book and worked the sum for him:

$$\begin{array}{r} 365 \\ \underline{\quad 1} \\ 364 \end{array}$$

Humpty Dumpty took the book, and looked at it carefully. "That seems to be right—" he began.

"You're holding it upside down!" Alice interrupted.

"To be sure I was!" Humpty Dumpty said gaily, as she turned it round for him. "I thought it looked a little queer. As I was saying, that seems to be done right—though I haven't time to look it over thoroughly just now—and that shows that there are three hundred and sixty-four days when you might get un-birthday presents—"

"Certainly," said Alice.

"And only one for birthday presents, you know. There's glory for you!"

Contents

January 11

February 27

March 43

April 59

May 75

June 91

July 107

August 123

September 139

October 155

November 171

December 187

January

January 1

The sun was shining on the sea,
Shining with all his might:
He did his very best to make
The billows smooth and bright—
And this was odd, because it was
The middle of the night.

. . . .

. . . .

. . . .

January 2

The Lion and the Unicorn were fighting for the crown:
The Lion beat the Unicorn all round the town.

. . . .

. . . .

. . . .

♦ ♠

January 3

"Oh, how I wish I could shut up like a telescope!"

. . . .

. . . .

. . . .

January 4

"Do I look very pale?" said Tweedledum, coming up to have his helmet put on.

January 5

"The more head downwards I am, the more I keep inventing new things."

January 6

"I beg your pardon, your Majesty," he began, "for bringing these in, but I hadn't quite finished my tea when I was sent for."

January 7

The White Rabbit blew three blasts on the trumpet.

January 8

The King read out from his book "Rule Forty-two. *All persons more than a mile high to leave the court.*"

. . . .

. . . .

. . . .

♥ ♣

January 9

"Goodbye, feet! …Oh, my poor little feet!"

. . . .

. . . .

. . . .

January 10

The last time she saw them, they were trying to put the Dormouse into the teapot.

. . . .

. . . .

. . . .

January 11

"I can't stand this any longer!" she cried.

. . . .

. . . .

. . . .

January 12

"If everybody minded their own business," the Duchess said in a hoarse growl, "the world would go round a deal faster than it does."

January 13

The Hatter hurriedly left the court, without even waiting to put his shoes on.

January 14

They were standing under a tree, each with an arm round the other's neck...

. . . .

. . . .

. . . .

January 15

...Alice knew which was which in a moment, because one of them had "DUM" embroidered on his collar, and the other "DEE".

. . . .

. . . .

. . . .

January 16

"I mean, what is an un-birthday present?"
"A present given when it isn't your birthday, of course."

. . . .

. . . .

. . . .

January 17

Alice considered a little. "I like birthday presents best."

. . . .

. . . .

. . . .

January 18

"In *our* country," Alice remarked, "there's only one day at a time."

January 19

"Now! Now!" cried the Queen. "Faster! Faster!"

January 20

"Even if my head *would* go through," thought poor Alice, "it would be of very little use without my shoulders..."

January 21

"The rule is, jam to-morrow and jam yesterday – but never jam today."

January 22

Tweedledum and Tweedledee
Agreed to have a battle;

January 23

For Tweedledum said Tweedledee
Had spoiled his nice new rattle.

January 24

"Begin at the beginning," the King said gravely, "and go on till you come to the end: then stop."

. . . .

. . . .

. . . .

January 25

This time she found a little bottle ("which certainly was not here before," said Alice)...

. . . .

. . . .

. . . .

January 26

"I wonder who will put on your shoes and stockings for you now, dears?"

January 27

"O Tiger-lily! I *wish* you could talk."

January 28

'Twas brillig, and the slithy toves
Did gyre and gimble in the wabe...

January 29

All mimsy were the borogoves,
And the mome raths outgrabe.

January 30

…round its neck a paper label, with the words "DRINK ME" beautifully printed on it in large letters.

. . . .

. . . .

. . . .

January 31

Still she went on growing, and, as a last resource,
she put one arm out of the window,
and one foot up the chimney…

. . . .

. . . .

. . . .

February

February 1

She tried the little golden key in the lock, and to her great delight it fitted.

. . . .

. . . .

. . . .

February 2

"I'm afraid you've not had much practice in riding," Alice ventured to say…

. . . .

. . . .

. . . .

February 3

"You alarm me!" said the King.
"I feel faint – Give me a ham-sandwich!"

. . . .

. . . .

. . . .

February 4

The Caterpillar and Alice looked at each
other for some time in silence.

. . . .

. . . .

. . . .

February 5

Alice felt so desperate that she was ready
to ask help of anyone;

. . . .

. . . .

. . . .

February 6

…she began, in a low, timid voice,
"If you please, sir—"

. . . .

. . . .

. . . .

February 7

He came in with a teacup in one hand and a piece of bread-and-butter in the other.

. . . .

. . . .

. . . .

February 8

She did not get hold of anything, but she heard a little shriek and a fall, and a crash of broken glass…

. . . .

. . . .

. . . .

February 9

"Poor little thing!" said Alice, in a coaxing tone…

February 10

…she picked up a little bit of stick,
and held it out to the puppy.

February 11

They very soon came upon a Gryphon,
lying fast asleep in the sun.

February 12

"...and the moral of that is— 'Take care of the sense, and the sounds will take care of themselves.'"

February 13

"You seem very clever at explaining words, Sir," said Alice.

. . . .

. . . .

. . . .

February 14

"Well! I've often seen a cat without a grin," thought Alice, "but a grin without a cat! It's the most curious thing I ever saw in all my life!"

. . . .

. . . .

. . . .

February 15

"Contrariwise," continued Tweedledee, "if it was so, it might be; and if it were so, it would be: but as it isn't, it ain't. That's logic."

. . . .

. . . .

. . . .

♥ ♣

February 16

"There's certainly too much pepper in that soup!"

. . . .

. . . .

. . . .

February 17

"Why did you call him Tortoise, if he wasn't one?" Alice asked.

. . . .

. . . .

. . . .

February 18

"We called him Tortoise because he taught us," said the Mock Turtle angrily; "really you are very dull!"

. . . .

. . . .

. . . .

February 19

At last the Dodo said, "*Everybody* has won, and *all* must have prizes."

February 20

. . . in his confusion he bit a large piece out of his tea-cup instead of the bread-and-butter.

February 21

The moon was shining sulkily,

Because she thought the sun…

February 22

Had got no business to be there

After the day was done—

February 23

"Ahem!" said the Mouse with an important air, "are you all ready?"

February 24

. . . she gave one sharp kick, and waited to see what would happen next.

February 25

The Rabbit started violently, dropped the white kid gloves and the fan, and scurried away into the darkness as hard as he could go.

. . . .

. . . .

. . . .

February 26

"...I should like to be a *little* larger, sir, if you wouldn't mind," said Alice: "three inches is such a wretched height to be."

. . . .

. . . .

. . . .

February 27

…she concluded that it was just possible it might have fallen into a cucumber frame, or something of the sort.

. . . .

. . . .

. . . .

February 28

"If you're going to turn into a pig, my dear," said Alice, seriously, "I'll have nothing more to do with you."

. . . .

. . . .

. . . .

February 29

"'Be what you would seem to be'—or, if you'd like it put more simply—'Never imagine yourself not to be otherwise than what it might appear to others that what you were or might have been was not otherwise than what you had been would have appeared to them to be otherwise.'"

. . . .

. . . .

. . . .

♦ ♠

March

March 1

Twinkle, twinkle, little bat!
How I wonder what you're at!
Up above the world you fly,
Like a tea-tray in the sky.

. . . .

. . . .

. . . .

March 2

"I wish they'd get the trial done," she thought, "and hand round the refreshments!"

. . . .

. . . .

. . . .

March 3

"And what is the use of a book," thought Alice, "without pictures or conversation?"

. . . .

. . . .

. . . .

March 4

"Would you tell me, please, which way I ought to go from here?"

. . . .

. . . .

. . . .

♥ ♣

March 5

"That depends a good deal on where you want to get to," said the Cat.

. . . .

. . . .

. . . .

March 6

"Curiouser and curiouser!" cried Alice; "now I'm opening out like the largest telescope that ever was!"

March 7

"Give your evidence," said the King; "and don't be nervous, or I'll have you executed on the spot."

March 8

"I told you butter wouldn't suit the works," he added, looking angrily at the March Hare.

. . . .

. . . .

. . . .

♥ ♣

March 9

"It was the *best* butter," the March Hare meekly replied.

. . . .

. . . .

. . . .

March 10

...they went so fast that at last they seemed to skim through the air.

. . . .

. . . .

. . . .

♦ ♠

March 11

"Well! *What* are you?" said the Pigeon. "I can see you're trying to invent something!"

. . . .

. . . .

. . . .

March 12

The Cat only grinned when it saw Alice.

March 13

"You ought to have finished," said the King. "When did you begin?"

March 14

"Fourteenth of March, I *think* it was."

. . . .

. . . .

. . . .

♦ ♠

March 15

"Fifteenth," said the March Hare.

. . . .

. . . .

. . . .

March 16

"Sixteenth," added the Dormouse.

March 17

"I'm doubtful about the temper of your flamingo."

March 18

The first thing she heard was a general chorus of, "There goes Bill!"

. . . .

. . . .

. . . .

March 19

"Catch him, you by the hedge!"

. . . .

. . . .

. . . .

March 20

"No room! No room!" they cried out
when they saw Alice coming.

March 21

In spring, when woods are getting green,
I'll try and tell you what I mean:

March 22

He said, "I look for butterflies
That sleep among the wheat;

March 23

"I make them into mutton pies,
And sell them in the street."

March 24

…the glass was beginning to melt away, just like a bright silvery mist.

. . . .

. . . .

. . . .

March 25

"In that direction," the Cat said, waving its right paw round, "lives a Hatter; and in that direction," waving the other paw, "lives a March Hare."

. . . .

. . . .

. . . .

March 26

"I don't much care where… so long as I get somewhere."

March 27

"…you're sure to do that," said the Cat, "if you only walk long enough."

March 28

"Oh my dear paws! Oh my fur and whiskers!"

March 29

Alice soon came to the conclusion it was a very difficult game indeed.

March 30

"For the Duchess. An invitation from the Queen to play croquet."

March 31

"From the Queen. An invitation for the Duchess to play croquet."

April

April 1

Her first idea was that she had somehow fallen into the sea…

. . . .

. . . .

. . . .

♦ ♠

April 2

"and in that case, I can go back by railway," she said to herself.

. . . .

. . . .

. . . .

April 3

"Who are you, aged man?" I said
"And how is it you live?"

April 4

And his answer trickled through my head
Like water through a sieve.

April 5

"There's *plenty* of room!" said Alice indignantly...

April 6

It flashed across her mind that she had never before seen a rabbit with either a waist-coat pocket, or a watch to take out of it.

April 7

"If you knew time as well as I do," said the Hatter, "you wouldn't talk about wasting *it*. It's *him*."

April 8

"Hold your tongue!" said the Queen, turning purple.
"I won't!" said Alice.

April 9

"You are old, Father William," the young man said,
"And your hair has become very white:"

April 10

"And yet you incessantly stand on your head—
Do you think at your age, it is right?"

April 11

"I don't know what you mean," said Alice.

. . . .

. . . .

. . . .

April 12

"Why, the fact is, you see, miss, this here ought to have been a *red* rose tree, and we put a white one in by mistake—"

. . . .

. . . .

. . . .

April 13

"I dare say you never even spoke to Time!"

. . . .

. . . .

. . . .

♦ ♠

April 14

"…I know I have to beat time when I learn music."

. . . .

. . . .

. . . .

April 15

[Alice] looked back once or twice, half hoping that they would call after her…

. . . .

. . . .

. . . .

April 16

The King and Queen of Hearts were seated on their throne.

. . . .

. . . .

. . . .

April 17

"The time has come," the Walrus said,
"To talk of many things:"

April 18

"Of shoes—and ships—and sealing-wax—
Of cabbages—and kings—"

April 19

"Smooth her hair—lend her your night-cap and sing her a soothing lullaby."

. . . .

. . . .

. . . .

April 20

"Now the reason hair falls off is because it hangs *down*—things never fall *upwards*, you know."

. . . .

. . . .

. . . .

April 21

"Can you do Division? Divide a loaf by a knife —what's the answer to *that*?"

. . . .

. . . .

. . . .

April 22

"Try another Subtraction sum.
Take a bone from a dog: what remains?"

. . . .

. . . .

. . . .

April 23

Then fill up the glasses as quick as you can,
And sprinkle the table with buttons and bran:

. . . .

. . . .

. . . .

April 24

Put cats in the coffee, and mice in the tea—
And welcome Queen Alice with thirty-times-three!

. . . .

. . . .

. . . .

April 25

And as in uffish thought he stood,
The Jabberwock, with eyes of flame…

. . . .

. . . .

. . . .

April 26

Came whiffling through the tulgey wood,
And burbled as it came!

. . . .

. . . .

. . . .

April 27

Alice had been to the seaside once in her life…

. . . .

. . . .

. . . .

April 28

…she soon made out that she was in the pool of tears that she had wept when she was nine feet high.

. . . .

. . . .

. . . .

April 29

"Really, now you ask me," said Alice, very much confused, "I don't think—"

"Then you shouldn't talk," said the Hatter.

. . . .

. . . .

. . . .

April 30

She generally gave herself very good advice (though she very seldom followed it).

. . . .

. . . .

. . . .

May

May 1

Speak roughly to your little boy,
And beat him when he sneezes;
He only does it to annoy,
Because he know it teases.

. . . .

. . . .

. . . .

May 2

Alice had not the slightest idea what Latitude was, or Longitude either, but she thought they were nice grand words to say.

. . . .

. . . .

. . . .

May 3

"The different branches of Arithmetic—Ambition, Distraction, Uglification and Derision."

. . . .

. . . .

. . . .

May 4

"You don't know how to manage Looking-glass cakes," the Unicorn remarked. "Hand it round first, and cut it afterwards."

. . . .

. . . .

. . . .

May 5

She had never forgotten that, if you drink from a bottle marked "poison", it is almost certain to disagree with you, sooner or later.

. . . .

. . . .

. . . .

May 6

"We *can* talk," said the Tigerlily: "when there's anybody worth talking to."

. . . .

. . . .

. . . .

May 7

"In most gardens," the Tigerlily said, "they make the beds too soft—so that the flowers are always asleep."

. . . .

. . . .

. . . .

May 8

"It's the oldest rule in the book," said the King.
"Then it ought to be Number One," said Alice.

May 9

"If you do such a thing again, I'll have you buttered!"

May 10

"I'm brave generally," he went on in a low voice: "only to-day I happen to have a headache."

. . . .

. . . .

. . . .

May 11

"They're dreadfully fond of beheading people here: the great wonder is that there's anyone left alive!"

. . . .

. . . .

. . . .

May 12

"I can't help it," said Alice very meekly: "I'm growing."
"You've no right to grow here," said the Dormouse.

. . . .

. . . .

. . . .

May 13

"I can't go no lower," said the Hatter:
"I'm on the floor, as it is."

. . . .

. . . .

. . . .

May 14

How doth the little crocodile
Improve his shining tail,
And pour the waters of the Nile
On every golden scale!

. . . .

. . . .

. . . .

May 15

"The other Messenger's called Hatta.
I must have *two*, you know—to come and go.
One to come, and one to go."

. . . .

. . . .

May 16

"Mine is a long and a sad tale!" said the Mouse, turning to Alice and sighing.

. . . .

. . . .

. . . .

May 17

"It *is* a long tail, certainly," said Alice… "but why do you call it sad?"

. . . .

. . . .

. . . .

May 18

Humpty Dumpty sat on a wall:
Humpty Dumpty had a great fall

May 19

All the King's horses and all the King's men
Couldn't put Humpty in his place again.

May 20

"Once," said the Mock Turtle at last, with a deep sigh, "I was a real Turtle."

May 21

"You're enough to try the patience of an oyster!"

May 22

"It'll never do for you to be lolling about on the grass like that! Queens have to be dignified, you know!"

. . . .

. . . .

. . . .

May 23

"I beg your pardon?" said Alice.
"It isn't respectable to beg," said the King.

. . . .

. . . .

. . . .

May 24

"Who are you?" said the Caterpillar. This was not an encouraging opening for a conversation.

. . . .

. . . .

. . . .

♥ ♣

May 25

The Caterpillar and Alice looked at each other for some time in silence.

. . . .

. . . .

. . . .

May 26

"Speak in French when you can't think of the English for a thing—turn out your toes as you walk—and remember who you are!"

. . . .

. . . .

. . . .

May 27

"I can't explain *myself*, I'm afraid, Sir," said Alice, "because I'm not myself, you see."

. . . .

. . . .

. . . .

May 28

The sea was wet as wet could be,
The sands were dry as dry.

May 29

You could not see a cloud, because
No cloud was in the sky:

May 30

"How do you know I'm mad?" said Alice.
"You must be," said the Cat, "or you wouldn't have come here."

. . . .

. . . .

. . . .

May 31

"Well, then," the Cat went on, "you see a dog growls when it's angry, and wags its tail when it's pleased. Now *I* growl when I'm pleased, and wag my tail when I'm angry. Therefore I'm mad."

. . . .

. . . .

June

June 1

"You can really have no notion how delightful it will be when they take us up and throw us, with the lobsters, out to sea!"

June 2

"I think you might do something better with time," [Alice] said, "than wasting it in asking riddles that have no answers."

June 3

"Let's fight till six, and then have dinner," said Tweedledum.

. . . .

. . . .

. . . .

June 4

"Four times round is enough for one dance," Tweedledum panted…

. . . .

. . . .

. . . .

June 5

"I *am* real!" said Alice, and began to cry.
"You won't make yourself a bit realer by crying,"
Tweedledee remarked: "there's nothing to cry about."

. . . .

. . . .

. . . .

June 6

"I—I'm a little girl," said Alice, rather doubtfully,
as she remembered the number of changes
she had gone through that day.

. . . .

. . . .

. . . .

June 7

For I holds it like glue—
Holds the lid to the dish, while it lies in the middle:

June 8

Which is easiest to do,
Un-dish-cover the fish or dishcover the riddle?

June 9

"So young a child," said the gentleman sitting opposite to her, "ought to know which way she's going, even if she doesn't know her own name!"

June 10

"I can't stand this any longer!" she cried.

June 11

"If everybody minded their own business," the Duchess said in a hoarse growl, "the world would go round a deal faster than it does."

. . . .

. . . .

. . . .

June 12

"I shouldn't know you again if we *did* meet… you're so exactly like other people."

. . . .

. . . .

. . . .

June 13

"It's as large as life and twice as natural!"

June 14

"Good-bye feet!" (for when she looked down at her feet, they seemed to be almost out of sight).

June 15

"And hast thou slain the Jabberwock?
Come to my arms, my beamish boy!

June 16

"O frabjous day! Callooh! Callay!"
He chortled in his joy.

June 17

"Let the jury consider their verdict," the King said... "No, no!" said the Queen. "Sentence first— verdict afterwards."

. . . .

. . . .

. . . .

June 18

The King's argument was that anything that had a head could be beheaded, and that you weren't to talk nonsense.

. . . .

. . . .

. . . .

June 19

"There's a large mustard-mine near here. And the moral of that is—'The more there is of mine, the less there is of yours'."

. . . .

. . . .

. . . .

June 20

"Flamingoes and mustard both bite. And the moral of that is— 'Birds of a feather flock together'."

. . . .

. . . .

. . . .

June 21

In summer, when the days are long,
Perhaps you'll understand the song.

. . . .

. . . .

. . . .

♦ ♠

June 22

"When we were little, we went to school in the sea."

. . . .

. . . .

. . . .

June 23

The Queen of Hearts, she made some tarts,
All on a summer day:

June 24

The Knave of Hearts, he stole those tarts
And took them quite away!

June 25

"I didn't know that Cheshire-Cats always grinned; in fact, I didn't know that cats *could* grin."

June 26

"They all can," said the Duchess; "and most of 'em do."

June 27

"O Looking-Glass creature," quoth Alice, "draw near!"
'Tis an honour to see me, a favour to hear:

. . . .

. . . .

. . . .

♥ ♣

June 28

"'Tis a privilege high to have dinner and tea
Along with the Red Queen, the White Queen, and me!"

. . . .

. . . .

June 29

"Who cares for *you*?" said Alice. "You're nothing but a pack of cards!"

. . . .

. . . .

. . . .

June 30

"Don't grunt," said Alice; "that's not at all a proper way of expressing yourself."

. . . .

. . . .

. . . .

July

July 1

A boat, beneath a sunny sky,
Lingering onward dreamily
In an evening of July—

. . . .

. . . .

. . . .

July 2

"In my youth," Father William replied to his son,
"I feared it might injure the brain;

. . . .

. . . .

. . . .

July 3

"But, now that I'm perfectly sure I have none,
Why, I do it again and again."

. . . .

. . . .

. . . .

July 4

All in the golden afternoon
Full leisurely we glide;

July 5

"I wish *I* could manage to be glad!" the Queen said. "Only I never can remember the rule."

July 6

"What matters it how far we go?"
his scaly friend replied,
"There is another shore, you know,
upon the other side."

. . . .

. . . .

July 7

"The further off from England
the nearer is to France—
Then turn not pale, beloved snail,
but come and join the dance."

. . . .

. . . .

July 8

"You see the earth takes twenty-four hours
to turn on its axis—"
"Talking of axes," said the Duchess,
"chop off her head!"

. . . .

. . . .

July 9

"Now, I give you fair warning," shouted the Queen;
"either you or your head must be off, and that in about
half no time! Take your choice!"

. . . .

. . . .

. . . .

July 10

There was a pause in the fight just then, and the Lion and the Unicorn sat down, panting, while the King called out, "Ten minutes for refreshments!"

. . . .

. . . .

. . . .

July 11

"Collar that Dormouse!" the Queen shrieked out. "Behead that Dormouse! Turn that Dormouse out of the court! Suppress him! Pinch him! Off with his whiskers!"

. . . .

. . . .

. . . .

July 12

I shook him well from side to side,
Until his face was blue:

July 13

"Come, tell me how you live," I cried.
"And what it is you do!"

July 14

"Perhaps you were never even introduced to a lobster… so you can have no idea what a delightful thing a Lobster-Quadrille is?"

July 15

"What *is* a Caucus-race?" said Alice;
not that she much wanted to know…
"Why," said the Dodo,
"the best way to explain it is to do it."

July 16

But I was thinking of a plan
To dye one's whiskers green,

July 17

And always use so large a fan
That they could not be seen.

July 18

"I'm sure I'm not Ada," she said, "for her hair goes in such long ringlets, and mine doesn't go in ringlets at all;"

. . . .

. . . .

. . . .

♦ ♠

July 19

"…and I'm sure I can't be Mabel, for I know all sorts of things, and she, oh, she knows such a very little!"

. . . .

. . . .

. . . .

July 20

One, two! One, two! And through and through
The vorpal blade went snicker-snack!

July 21

He left it dead, and with its head
He went galumphing back.

July 22

"I don't like belonging to another person's dream."

. . . .

. . . .

. . . .

July 23

"Well, now that we have seen each other," said the Unicorn, "if you'll believe in me, I'll believe in you. Is that a bargain?"

. . . .

. . . .

. . . .

July 24

"It is very provoking," Humpty Dumpty said after a long silence, looking away from Alice as he spoke, "to be called an egg—very!"

. . . .

. . . .

. . . .

July 25

"My name means the shape I am—
and a good handsome shape it is, too."

. . . .

. . . .

. . . .

July 26

It was so long since she had been anything near the right size, that it felt quite strange at first.

. . . .

. . . .

. . . .

July 27

"I never ask advice about growing," Alice said indignantly.

. . . .

. . . .

. . . .

July 28

"Take off your hat," the King said to the Hatter.
"It isn't mine," said the Hatter.
"*Stolen!*" the King exclaimed.

. . . .

. . . .

. . . .

July 29

"Where are you going? Look up, speak nicely,
and don't twiddle your fingers all the time."

. . . .

. . . .

. . . .

July 30

He took his vorpal sword in hand:
Long time the manxome foe he sought—

July 31

So rested he by the Tumtum tree,
And stood a while in thought.

August

August 1

"Will you walk a little faster?" said a whiting to a snail.
"There's a porpoise close behind us,
and he's treading on my tail.
See how eagerly the lobsters and
the turtles all advance!
They are waiting on the shingle—
will you come and join the dance?"

August 2

"Are you a child or a teetotum?" the Sheep said, as she took up another pair of needles.

August 3

"Oh, I've had such a curious dream!" said Alice.

August 4

"You are old," said the youth;
"one would hardly suppose
That your eye was as steady as ever;"

August 5

"Yet you balanced an eel on the end of your nose—
What made you so awfully clever?"

August 6

"No wise fish would go anywhere without a porpoise."

August 7

"I can repeat poetry as well as other
folk if it comes to that—"
"Oh, it needn't come to that!" Alice hastily said.

August 8

"She ought to know her way to the ticket-office, even if she doesn't know her alphabet!"

. . . .

. . . .

. . . .

August 9

"You should learn not to make personal remarks," Alice said with some severity: "it's very rude."

. . . .

. . . .

. . . .

August 10

And now, if e'er by chance I put
My fingers into glue,

. . . .

. . . .

. . . .

♦ ♠

August 11

Or madly squeeze a right-hand foot
Into a left-hand shoe…

. . . .

. . . .

. . . .

August 12

"A little kindness—and putting her hair in papers would do wonders with her—"

August 13

"Consider what a great girl you are… Consider what o'clock it is. Consider anything, only don't cry!"

August 14

The Lion looked at Alice wearily. "Are you an animal or vegetable—or mineral?" he said.

. . . .

. . . .

. . . .

♦ ♠

August 15

"I suppose you don't want to lose your name?"
"No, indeed," Alice said, a little anxiously.

. . . .

. . . .

. . . .

August 16

"That's the reason they're called lessons," the Gryphon remarked: "because they lessen from day to day."

. . . .

. . . .

. . . .

August 17

"I don't know the meaning of half those long words, and, what's more, I don't believe you do either!"

. . . .

. . . .

. . . .

August 18

"This conversation is going on a little too fast:
let's go back to the last remark but one."

. . . .

. . . .

. . . .

August 19

"Another sandwich!" said the King;
"There's nothing but hay left now," the Messenger said,
peeping into the bag.
"Hay, then," the King murmured in a faint whisper.

. . . .

. . . .

. . . .

August 20

"I have answered three questions, and that is enough,"
Said his father; "don't give yourself airs!"

August 21

"Do you think I can listen all day to such stuff?
Be off, or I'll kick you downstairs!"

August 22

"You look a little shy: let me introduce you to that leg of mutton," said the Red Queen.

. . . .

. . . .

. . . .

August 23

"Take some more tea," the March Hare said to Alice, very earnestly.

"I've had nothing yet," Alice replied in an offended tone, "so I can't take more."

. . . .

. . . .

. . . .

August 24

"I'm sure nobody walks much faster than I do!"
"He can't do that," said the King,
"or else he'd have been here first."

. . . .

. . . .

. . . .

August 25

In another moment Alice was through the glass, and had jumped lightly down into the Looking-glass room.

. . . .

. . . .

. . . .

August 26

"Curtsey while you're thinking what to say. It saves time."

. . . .

. . . .

. . . .

August 27

"I assure you, my dear, I turned cold to the very ends of my whiskers!"

. . . .

. . . .

. . . .

August 28

"What's the French for fiddle-de-dee?"
"Fiddle-de-dee's not English," Alice replied.

August 29

"You don't know much," said the Duchess;
"and that's a fact."

August 30

"Did you ever see such a thing as a drawing of a muchness?"

. . . .

. . . .

. . . .

August 31

"I can read words of one letter! Isn't *that* grand? However, don't be discouraged. You'll come to it in time."

. . . .

. . . .

. . . .

September

September 1

For "happy summer days" gone by,
And vanish'd summer glory—

September 2

It shall not touch, with breath of bale,
The pleasance of our fairy-tale.

September 3

"Why, sometimes I've believed as many as
six impossible things before breakfast."

. . . .

. . . .

. . . .

♥ ♣

September 4

"Always speak the truth— think before you speak—
and write it down afterwards."

. . . .

. . . .

. . . .

September 5

"Now the cleverest thing that I ever did," he went on after a pause, "was inventing a new pudding during the meat-course!"

. . . .

. . . .

. . . .

♦ ♠

September 6

"Are their heads off?" shouted the Queen.

. . . .

. . . .

. . . .

September 7

In a Wonderland they lie,
Dreaming as the days go by,

September 8

Dreaming as the summers die;

September 9

"Fan her head!" the Red Queen anxiously interrupted. "She'll be feverish after so much thinking."

September 10

Stooping down to the daisies, who were just beginning again, she whispered, "If you don't hold your tongues, I'll pick you!"

September 11

"You see it's like a portmanteau—
there are two meanings packed up into one word."

. . . .

. . . .

. . . .

September 12

"How am I to get in?" asked Alice again, in a louder tone.
"*Are* you to get in at all?" said the Footman.
"That's the first question, you know."

. . . .

. . . .

. . . .

September 13

To the Looking-Glass world it was Alice that said,
"I've a sceptre in hand, I've a crown on my head."

. . . .

. . . .

. . . .

September 14

"Let the Looking-Glass creatures, whatever they be,
Come and dine with the Red Queen,
the White Queen, and me!"

. . . .

. . . .

. . . .

September 15

"Never mind what they all say, my dear, but take a return-ticket every time the train stops."

. . . .

. . . .

. . . .

September 16

"Pudding—Alice: Alice—Pudding. Remove the pudding!" and the waiters took it away so quickly that Alice couldn't return its bow.

. . . .

. . . .

. . . .

September 17

She opened it, and found in it a very small cake, on which the words "EAT ME" were beautifully marked in currants.

. . . .

. . . .

. . . .

September 18

The Dodo solemnly presented the thimble, saying, "We beg your acceptance of this elegant thimble."

. . . .

. . . .

. . . .

September 19

"Then you should say what you mean,"
the March Hare went on.
"I do," Alice hastily replied; "at least—at least I mean
what I say—that's the same thing, you know."

. . . .

. . . .

September 20

"Not the same thing a bit!" said the Hatter. "Why, you
might just as well say that 'I see what I eat'
is the same thing as 'I eat what I see'!"

. . . .

. . . .

. . . .

September 21

In autumn, when the leaves are brown,
Take pen and ink, and write it down.

. . . .

. . . .

. . . .

♦ ♠

September 22

"The Drawling-master was an old conger-eel… *he* taught us Drawling, Stretching and Fainting in Coils."

. . . .

. . . .

. . . .

September 23

Long has paled that sunny sky;
Echoes fade and memories die:

September 24

Autumn frosts have slain July.

September 25

"What sort of things do you remember best?" Alice ventured to ask.

"Oh, things that happened the week after next," the Queen replied in a careless tone.

September 26

"He's an Anglo-Saxon Messenger—and those are Anglo-Saxon attitudes."

September 27

The Queen bawled out "He's murdering the time! Off with his head!"

September 28

"It was much pleasanter at home," thought poor Alice, "when one wasn't always growing larger and smaller, and being ordered about by mice and rabbits."

September 29

Ever drifting down the stream—
Lingering in the golden gleam—

. . . .

. . . .

. . . .

♦ ♠

September 30

Life, what is it, but a dream?

. . . .

. . . .

. . . .

October

October 1

"'Tis the voice of the lobster: I heard him declare
'You have baked me too brown, I must sugar my hair.'"
As a duck with its eyelids, so he with his nose
Trims his belt and his buttons, and turns out his toes.

. . . .

. . . .

. . . .

October 2

Down, down, down.
Would the fall *never* come to an end?

October 3

"If there's no meaning in it," said the King,
"that saves a world of trouble, you know,
as we needn't try to find any."

October 4

"Come, fetch the plum-cake, old man!" the Unicorn went on, turning from Alice to the King. "None of your brown bread for me!"

. . . .

. . . .

. . . .

October 5

"Let's pretend the glass has got soft like gauze so that we can get through."

. . . .

. . . .

. . . .

October 6

"You know," he added gravely, "it's one of the most serious things that can possibly happen to one in a battle—to get one's head cut off."

. . . .

. . . .

. . . .

October 7

"What's the use of their having names," the Gnat said, "if they won't answer to them?"

. . . .

. . . .

. . . .

October 8

"There's nothing like eating hay when you're faint."

October 9

But answer came there none—
And this was scarcely odd, because
They'd eaten every one.

October 10

"You may look in front of you, and on both sides, if you like," said the Sheep; "but you can't look *all* round you—unless you've got eyes at the back of your head."

. . . .

. . . .

. . . .

October 11

"I cried, 'Come, tell me how you live!'
And thumped him on the head."

. . . .

. . . .

. . . .

October 12

"I don't deny things with my *hands*," Alice objected. "Nobody said you did," said the Red Queen, "I said you couldn't if you tried."

. . . .

. . . .

. . . .

♥ ♣

October 13

"How fast those Queens *can* run!"

. . . .

. . . .

. . . .

October 14

"It's time for you to answer now," the Queen said, looking at her watch: "open your mouth a *little* wider when you speak, and always say, 'your Majesty'."

. . . .

. . . .

. . . .

October 15

"Some people," said Humpty Dumpty… "Have no more sense than a baby!"

. . . .

. . . .

. . . .

October 16

The players all played at once without waiting for turns, quarrelling all the while, and fighting for hedgehogs.

October 17

"That's the effect of living backwards."

October 18

"Speak only when you're spoken to!" the Queen sharply interrupted her.

. . . .

. . . .

. . . .

October 19

"But if everybody obeyed that rule," said Alice… "and if you only spoke when you were spoken to, and the other person always waited for *you* to begin, you see nobody would ever say anything…"

. . . .

. . . .

. . . .

October 20

She tried the little golden key in the lock, and to her great delight it fitted!

. . . .

. . . .

. . . .

October 21

The Queen turned crimson with fury, and, after glaring at her for a moment like a wild beast, screamed, "Off with her head!"

. . . .

. . . .

. . . .

October 22

The Red Queen shook her head. "You may call it 'nonsense' if you like," she said, "but I've heard nonsense, compared with which that would be as sensible as a dictionary!"

. . . .

. . . .

. . . .

October 23

"When I make a word do a lot of work like that," said Humpty Dumpty, "I always pay it extra."

. . . .

. . . .

. . . .

October 24

The confusion got worse every moment.

October 25

Alice jumped in such a hurry that she tipped over the jury-box with the edge of her skirt, upsetting all the jurymen on to the heads of the crowds below.

October 26

The executioner's argument was that you couldn't cut off a head unless there was a body to cut it off from.

. . . .

. . . .

. . . .

♦ ♠

October 27

When the feast's over, we'll go to the ball—
Red Queen, and White Queen, and Alice, and all!

. . . .

. . . .

. . . .

October 28

"Have you invented a plan for keeping the hair from being blown off?" Alice enquired.

"Not yet," said the Knight. "But I've got a plan for keeping it from *falling* off."

. . . .

. . . .

October 29

"What's one and one and one and one and one and one and one and one and one and one?"

"I don't know," said Alice. "I lost count."

. . . .

. . . .

. . . .

October 30

I gave her one, they gave him two,
You gave us three or more;

. . . .

. . . .

. . . .

♦ ♠

October 31

They all returned from him to you,
Though they were mine before.

. . . .

. . . .

. . . .

November

November 1

"If you think we're waxworks, you ought to pay, you know. Waxworks weren't made to be looked at for nothing. Nohow!"

November 2

"Queens never make bargains."

November 3

It had, in fact, a sort of mixed flavour of cherry-tart, custard, pine-apple, roast turkey, toffy, and hot buttered toast.

. . . .

. . . .

. . . .

November 4

"Oh, I liked it well enough… only it *was* so dusty and hot, and the elephants *did* tease so!"

. . . .

. . . .

. . . .

November 5

The Walrus and the Carpenter
Were walking close at hand;

November 6

They wept like anything to see
Such quantities of sand.

November 7

"He's in prison now, being punished, and the trial doesn't even begin till next Wednesday; and of course the crime comes last of all."

November 8

"She's *my* prisoner, you know!"
the Red Knight said at last.
"Yes, but then *I* came and rescued her!"
the White Knight replied.

November 9

"O Oysters, come and walk with us!"
The Walrus did beseech.

November 10

"A pleasant walk, a pleasant talk,
Along the briny beach."

November 11

Kitty sat very demurely on her knee, pretending to watch the progress of the winding, and now and then putting out one paw and gently touching the ball.

. . . .

. . . .

. . . .

♥ ♣

November 12

"The hairbrush has got entangled in it!" the Queen said with a sigh. "And I lost the comb yesterday."

. . . .

. . . .

. . . .

November 13

"What I was going to say," said the Dodo in an offended tone, "was that the best thing to get us dry would be a Caucus-race."

. . . .

. . . .

. . . .

November 14

"I am older than you, and must know better."

. . . .

. . . .

. . . .

November 15

"May I give you a slice?" Alice said.
"Certainly not," the Red Queen said, very decidedly:
"It isn't etiquette to cut any one you've been
introduced to."

. . . .

. . . .

. . . .

November 16

"You'll wait and wave your handkerchief when I get to that turn in the road? I think it'll encourage me, you see."

. . . .

. . . .

. . . .

November 17

"Well in *our* country," said Alice, still panting a little, "you'd generally get to somewhere else—if you ran very fast for a long time, as we've been doing."

November 18

"It's the stupidest tea-party I ever was at in all my life!"

November 19

"I want a clean cup," interrupted the Hatter: "let's all move one place on."

. . . .

. . . .

. . . .

November 20

"Four times five is twelve, and four times six is thirteen, and four times seven is—oh dear! I shall never get to twenty at that rate!"

. . . .

. . . .

. . . .

November 21

"I don't rejoice in insects at all," Alice explained, "because I'm rather afraid of them—at least the large kinds."

. . . .

. . . .

. . . .

♦ ♠

November 22

"Why is a raven like a writing-desk?"

. . . .

. . . .

. . . .

November 23

"My heart went hop, my heart went thump:
I filled the kettle at the pump."

November 24

She took down a jar from one of the shelves as she passed: it was labelled "ORANGE MARMALADE", but to her great disappointment it was empty.

November 25

"An arm, you goose! Who ever saw one that size?
Why, it fills the whole window!"
"Sure, it does, yer honour: but it's an arm for all that."

. . . .

. . . .

. . . .

November 26

"The daisies are worst of all. When one speaks, they all begin together, and it's enough to make one wither to hear the way they go on!"

. . . .

. . . .

. . . .

November 27

How cheerfully he seems to grin,
How neatly spreads his claws,

November 28

And welcomes little fishes in,
With gently smiling jaws!

November 29

Beware the Jabberwock, my son!
The jaws that bite, the claws that catch!

November 30

Beware the JubJub bird, and shun
The frumious Bandersnatch!

December

December 1

Beautiful Soup, so rich and green,
Waiting in a hot tureen!
Who for such dainties would not stoop?
Soup of the evening, beautiful Soup!

December 2

"The horror of that moment," the King went on,
"I shall never, *never* forget!"
"You will, though," the Queen said,
"if you don't make a memorandum of it."

. . . .

. . . .

. . . .

December 3

"*Why* do you say 'Feather' so often?" Alice asked at last, rather vexed. "I'm not a bird!"
"You are," said the Sheep: "you're a little goose."

. . . .

. . . .

. . . .

December 4

I speak severely to my boy,
I beat him when he sneezes;

December 5

For he can thoroughly enjoy
The pepper when he pleases!

December 6

"But it's no use now," thought poor Alice, "to pretend to be two people! Why, there's hardly enough of me left to make *one* respectable person!"

. . . .

. . . .

. . . .

December 7

"Don't keep him waiting child! Why, his time is worth a thousand pounds a minute!"

. . . .

. . . .

. . . .

December 8

"Why, I've done all the screaming already," said the Queen. "What would be the good of having it all over again?"

December 9

"Did you happen to meet any soldiers, my dear, as you came through the wood?"

"Yes, I did," said Alice: "several thousand, I should think."

December 10

"Now, Dinah, tell me the truth: did you ever eat a bat?"

. . . .

. . . .

. . . .

December 11

"I've a right to think," said Alice sharply, for she was beginning to feel a little worried.
"Just about as much right," said the Duchess, "as pigs have to fly."

. . . .

. . . .

. . . .

December 12

"My *name* is Alice, but—"
"It's a stupid name enough!" Humpty Dumpty interrupted impatiently. "What does it mean?"

. . . .

. . . .

. . . .

December 13

"You see the wind is so *very* strong here. It's as strong as soup."

. . . .

. . . .

. . . .

December 14

"In my youth," said his father, "I took to the law,
And argued each case with my wife;"

. . . .

. . . .

. . . .

♦ ♠

December 15

"And the muscular strength, which it gave to my jaw
Has lasted the rest of my life."

. . . .

. . . .

. . . .

December 16

"Little girls eat eggs quite as much as
serpents do, you know."
"I don't believe it," said the Pigeon; "but if they do,
why then they're a kind of serpent."

December 17

"Now, if you'll only attend, Kitty, and not talk so much,
I'll tell you all my ideas about Looking-glass House."

December 18

"One rule seems to be, that if one Knight hits the other, he knocks him off his horse; and, if he misses, he tumbles off himself."

. . . .

. . . .

. . . .

December 19

Another Rule of Battle, that Alice had not noticed, seemed to be that they always fell on their heads.

. . . .

. . . .

. . . .

December 20

"There's only one sword, you know," Tweedledum said to his brother; "but you can have the umbrella— it's quite as sharp."

December 21

In winter, when the fields are white,
I sing this song for your delight—

December 22

I said it very loud and clear:
I went and shouted in his ear.

. . . .

. . . .

. . . .

♦ ♠

December 23

Fancy *curtseying* as you're falling through the air!
Do you think you could manage it?

. . . .

. . . .

. . . .

December 24

Thus forgetting trick and play
For a moment, Lady dear,

December 25

We would wish you, if we may,
Merry Christmas, glad New Year!

December 26

"I make you a present of everything I've said as yet."

"A cheap sort of present!" thought Alice. "I'm glad they don't give birthday-presents like that!"

. . . .

. . . .

. . . .

December 27

Thus grew the tale of Wonderland:
Thus slowly, one by one...

. . . .

. . . .

. . . .

December 28

Its quaint events were hammered out—
And now the tale is done,

December 29

And home we steer, a merry crew,
Beneath the setting sun.

December 30

Alice thought to herself. "I don't see how he can ever finish, if he doesn't begin." But she waited patiently.

. . . .

. . . .

. . . .

December 31

Then fill up the glasses with treacle and ink,
Or anything else that is pleasant to drink:
Mix sand with the cider, and wool with the wine—
And welcome Queen Alice with ninety-times-nine!

. . . .

. . . .

. . . .

Other Alice titles from Macmillan Books

Alice's Adventures in Wonderland

By Lewis Carroll, illustrations by Sir John Tenniel

Hardback edition

ISBN 978 1 4472 7308 0

Paperback edition

ISBN 978 1 4472 7999 0

Through the Looking-Glass and What Alice Found There

By Lewis Carroll, illustrations by Sir John Tenniel

Hardback edition

ISBN 978 1 4472 73090 7

Paperback edition

ISBN 978 1 4472 8000 2

The Complete Alice

By Lewis Carroll, with illustrations by Sir John Tenniel in full colour

Foreword by Philip Pullman

ISBN 978 1 4472 7599 2

The Nursery Alice

By Lewis Carroll, illustrated by Sir John Tenniel

Cover designed and coloured by E Gertrude Thomson

ISBN 978 1 4472 8711 7

Alice's Adventures in Wonderland – The Little Folks Edition

By Lewis Carroll, illustrated by Sir John Tenniel

ISBN 978 1 4472 7778 1

What Would Alice Do?

Quotations from *Alice's Adventures in Wonderland* by Lewis Carroll

Illustrations by Sir John Tenniel

Foreword by Lauren Laverne

ISBN 978 1 4472 8852 7

100 Postcards from Wonderland

Lewis Carroll, with illustrations by Sir John Tenniel

ISBN 978 1 4472 9965 3

The Macmillan Alice: Mad Hatter Notebook
ISBN 978 1 5098 1041 3

The Macmillan Alice: White Rabbit Notebook
ISBN 978 1 5098 1040 6

Alice in Wonderland – Down the Rabbit Hole
Based on the classic tale by Lewis Carroll
Joe Rhatigan and Charles Nurnberg,
illustrated by Eric Puybaret
ISBN 978 1 4472 8623 3

Alice in Wonderland First Sticker Activity Book
Illustrated by Dan Taylor
ISBN 978 1 4472 8512 0

Alice in Wonderland Busy Board Book
Illustrated by Colonel Moutarde
ISBN 978 1 4472 7769 9

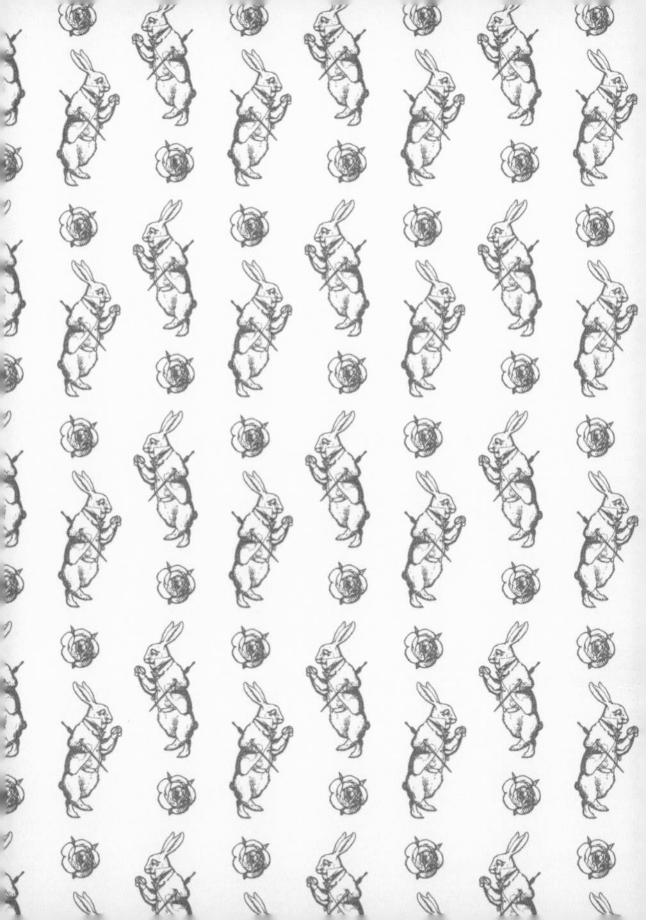

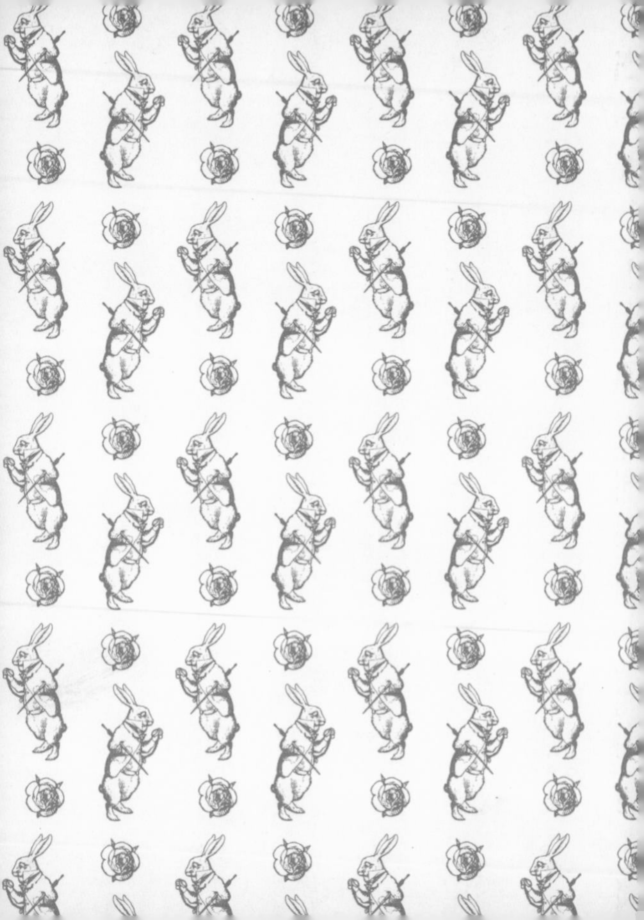